PICASSO
THE GREEN TREE FROG

For a free color catalog describing Gareth Stevens' list of high-quality books, call 1-800-542-2595 (USA) or 1-800-461-9120 (Canada). Gareth Stevens' Fax: (414) 225-0377.

Library of Congress Cataloging-in-Publication Data

Graham, Amanda, 1961-
  Picasso, the green tree frog.

  (A Quality time book)
  Summary: A green tree frog enjoys for a while the multicolored skin he acquires when he falls into a jar of jelly beans, but then he wishes for his familiar color back.
    [1. Tree frogs—fiction. 2. Frogs—fiction]
I. Siow, John, ill. II. Title.
PZ7.G751664Pi 1987 [E]   86-42809
ISBN 1-55532-152-6 (lib. bdg.)
ISBN 0-8368-1296-4 (trade)

North American edition first published in 1987 by
Gareth Stevens Publishing
1555 North RiverCenter Drive, Suite 201
Milwaukee, Wisconsin 53212, USA

Text © 1985 by Amanda Graham
Illustrations © 1985 by John Siow.

First published in Australia by Era Publications.

Typeset by A-Line Typographers, Milwaukee

Printed in the United States of America

4 5 6 7 8 9 99 98 97 96

PICASSO

THE GREEN

TREE FROG

Story by Amanda Graham
Pictures by John Siow

Gareth Stevens Publishing
Milwaukee

Picasso was a very clever
Green Tree Frog.

He could change color
by jumping
from here to there
and there to here
and back again.

Picasso could plop
into a muddy puddle
and turn brown.

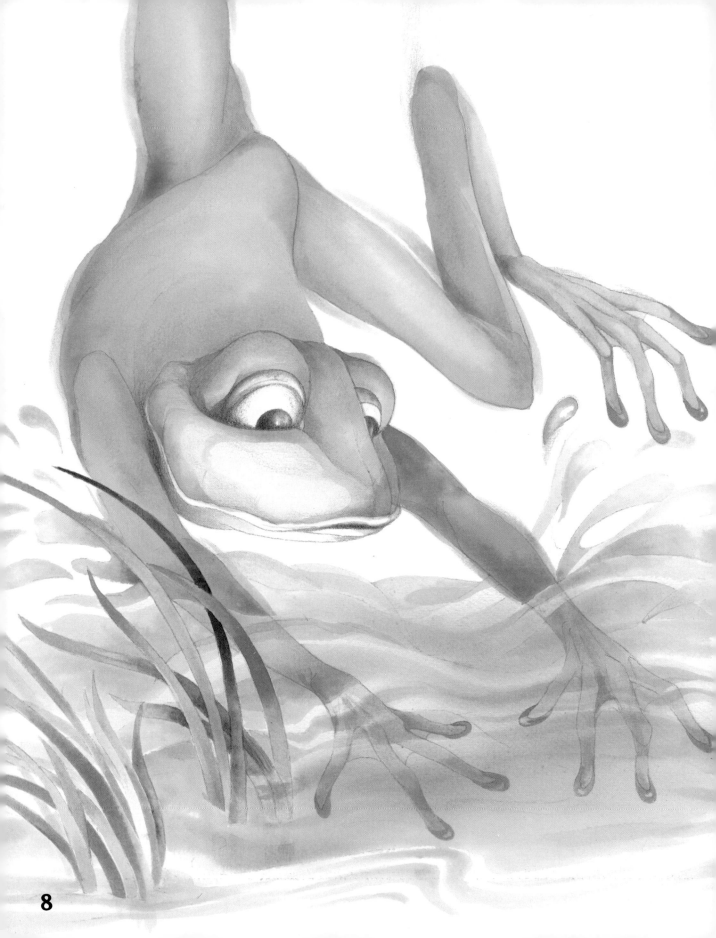

He could dive
into a deep, cool pool
and turn blue ...

9

and bounce back up
into his tree
to turn green again.

But one day,
as Picasso jumped from his tree,
something went wrong!

Picasso landed
in a jar of jellybeans
and turned all sorts of colors.

He enjoyed
being many colors
for a while.

But when he bounced back up
into his tree,
he did not turn green.

He slipped
into the lime-green slime ...
but still he did not turn green.

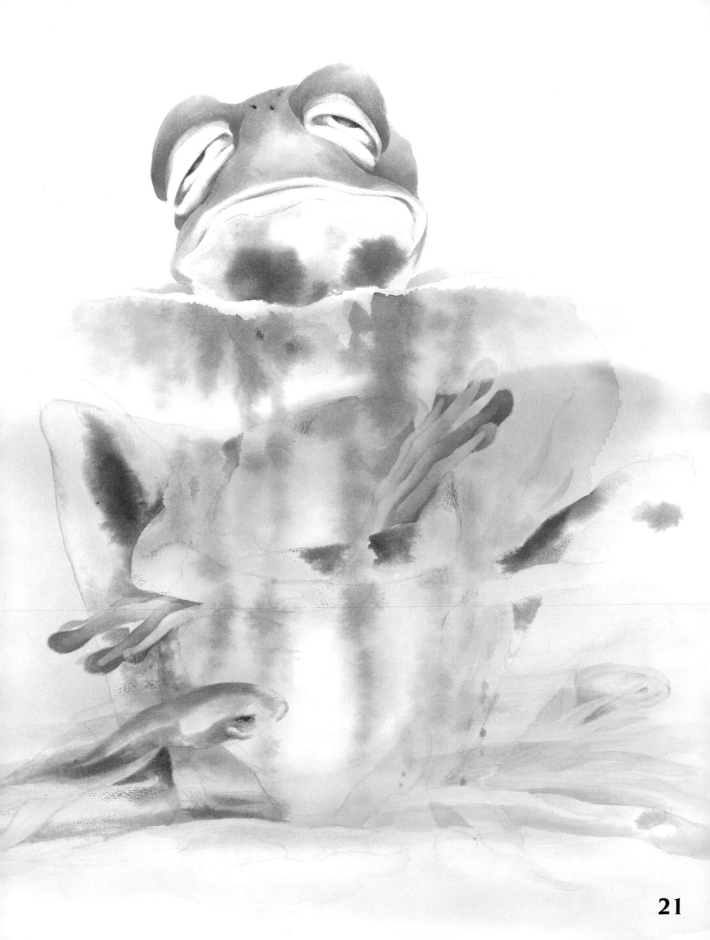

He wallowed in the watery weeds and reeds ...
but still he did not turn green.

There was no way, it seemed,
to become green again.

Picasso jumped back
to the jellybean jar.
He sighed
and tried
a pink jellybean.
He thought of
what to do next.
As he ate
another pink jellybean,
he noticed
something strange.

His pink spots had disappeared!
Picasso ate more jellybeans —
blue, red, yellow, purple,
every color
except green,
of course.

At last
he was himself again —
a green tree frog.

Or so he thought.